On Friday something funny happened

ALSO BY JOHN PRATER

You Can't Catch Me!
Along Came Tom
Timid Tim and the Cuggy Thief

For Julie, Jemma and Lauren

A Red Fox Book

Published by Random House Children's Books
20 Vauxhall Bridge Road, London SW1V 2SA

A division of Random House UK Ltd
London Melbourne Sydney Auckland
Johannesburg and agencies throughout the world

First published by The Bodley Head Children's
Books 1982

Red Fox edition 1993

5 7 9 10 8 6

© John Prater 1982

The right of John Prater to be identified as the
author and illustrator of this work has been
asserted by him in accordance with the Copyright,
Designs and Patents Act 1988.

Printed in China

RANDOM HOUSE UK Limited Reg. No. 954009

ISBN 0 09 918441 9

On Friday something funny happened

John Prater

RED FOX

On Saturday
we went shopping.

On Sunday
we went to the park.

On Monday
we did the washing.

On Tuesday
Uncle John came
to lunch.

On Wednesday
we did some painting.

On Thursday we played with our friends.

On Friday something funny happened— the house was very quiet.

On Saturday
we went shopping....

Some bestselling Red Fox picture books

THE BIG ALFIE AND ANNIE ROSE STORYBOOK
by Shirley Hughes
OLD BEAR
by Jane Hissey
OI! GET OFF OUR TRAIN
by John Burningham
I WANT A CAT
by Tony Ross
NOT NOW, BERNARD
by David McKee
ALL JOIN IN
by Quentin Blake
THE SAND HORSE
by Michael Foreman and Ann Turnbull
BAD BORIS GOES TO SCHOOL
by Susie Jenkin-Pearce
BILBO'S LAST SONG
by J.R.R. Tolkien
WILLY AND HUGH
by Anthony Browne
THE WINTER HEDGEHOG
by Ann and Reg Cartwright
A DARK, DARK TALE
by Ruth Brown
HARRY, THE DIRTY DOG
by Gene Zion and Margaret Bloy Graham
DR XARGLE'S BOOK OF EARTHLETS
by Jeanne Willis and Tony Ross
JAKE
by Deborah King